GRUFF GARRETT

THE OLD LAWDOG
NO WAY OUT

JOHN J. LAW

Chapter One: No Way Out

Gruff Garrett lay on the hard ground with his face looking up at the sky above him. He had a blank stare in his eyes and his companions weren't sure if he was still alive.

Alisa Pemberton and Paolo Dixon looked down upon Garrett and both of them were clearly concerned. Dixon was his long time rival and now prisoner, whom he was escorting back to a proper jail and trial. Alisa was the lady in waiting he had rescued earlier who had joined them. The old, black outlaw had always been warning Garrett that his gang was coming for him. He had said repeatedly that they were coming for him to make him pay for some old debts. Garrett never listened to Dixon, and now his gang was upon them. Apparently, the old lawdog had paid the price for ignoring the old outlaw's warning.

Bullets flew around them, but the young lady in waiting and the aging outlaw found shelter behind a rocky ridge and the walls of a cave at the top of the ledge they had climbed. The bullets flew around but hit the ledge, or the cave walls kicking up dust and pebbles but nothing more. Dixon's gang was just under them and firing up at them. Dixon clutched a rifle with both hands, and occasionally returned fire. Now seeing his old rival lying on the ground with a blank look in his face, it was a little harder for Dixon to concentrate on returning fire.

"Paolo, Gruff! He's... he's not breathing!" Alisa said.

"I can see that, girl! The old buzzard mentioned something about his having to take nitrogen pills or something like that to restart his heart! I can't really remember the specifics!"

"You think he has some of those pills on his person?"

Dixon looked at Alisa, and there was a look of desperation and panic in his eyes.

"Considering how we're here cornered an' trying to fight back against my old gang, it won't hurt to try and look around for them pills! I really don't know what else to do!" Dixon said.

He peeked from behind the ledge and fired another shot with his rifle. The shot cracked through the air, but

Dixon didn't hit any of the outlaws. There was still numerous boulders and some trees for them to hide behind.

Dixon took a look at the bottle of whiskey that Alisa had managed to bring up to the cave with them. It looked very appealing for the old man now.

"I sure could use some of that moonshine." he said.

Alisa ignored Dixon's desire for some moonshine as she began to frisk Garrett desperately. She checked his shirt pocket and found what she was looking for. Or at least it seemed like it. There were two pills in his shirt pocket. Alisa took them with her hand and held them up to the sunlight, as if they were a pair of gold nuggets.

"All right, these have to be the nitro pills for Garrett's heart. What else could they be?" she said.

Alisa still wasn't completely sure they were the right pills, but she couldn't hesitate. Gruff was lying on the ground, and she didn't really have any other options now. She opened his mouth and jammed both pills inside his mouth. She then massaged his throat to force the pills down.

Alisa looked at Garrett for several tense moments. He still wasn't moving, and it seemed as if the pills did not do their job.

Alisa didn't know how long she stared at the old marshal, and how long he lay on the ground. What she did know for sure was that he suddenly opened his eyes and began coughing.

"Gruff! Gruff!"

Alisa helped the old marshal to a sitting position. He was coughing and panting, but otherwise, he seemed to be all right.

"Alisa! I thought... I thought I was a goner... You found my pills. You saved me." he said.

"I didn't know what else to do, Gruff! I'm just glad you're still with us."

Alisa struggled to keep her voice from breaking. She couldn't help herself, and hugged Garrett. Garrett was surprised, but eventually smiled and held her, as well.

"It ain't this old lawdog's time yet, Alisa. All thanks to you. There was once a time I coulda climbed clear through without yer help in no time at all. But I was a younger man then, and well, it sure is a pain in the ass to get older!"

"Thanks for the compliment Gruff, but we still got ourselves a real pressing problem down below! If we don't address our problem, ain't none of us are gonna get any older!"

The sound of gunfire and the angry shouts of

the outlaws quickly snapped Gruff back to reality. For a moment, he had forgotten the dire situation that they were in.

"They're still below us! And from the sound of it, they want our blood real bad!"

Gruff turned towards Alisa and managed to get a good look at her. She looked haggard and exhausted. There was dirt and blood all over her hands, face and dress. Alisa looked much older than she really was, and looked more like someone who had been through a war than a lady in waiting. Garrett wasn't really surprised that she looked so bad. This was a small of sorts, after all.

"You all right, Alisa? You sure look like you've been

through the wringer." Gruff said.

"What did you expect, old man? We are in the middle of a gunfight here!"

"Good point."

Garrett turned and saw Dixon lying on the ground. His face was pressed to the ground and now, he was the one that wasn't moving.

"Good Lord, what happened to Dixon? Was he shot?"

Alisa shook her head. "Not that I noticed. He fell to the ground after taking in some moonshine."

Garrett slapped his forehead. "Of all the dumb and stupid things to do! Why am I not surprised? Wake up!"

Garrett pulled up Dixon's head and began slapping him with his palm. It took some slaps but the old outlaw finally came to his senses.

"What in tarnation? What's going on?" Dixon said.

"What's going on is, you're getting some shuteye at the worst possible time! Unless you forgot, we're under attack by your angry old friends!" Garrett said.

"Gruff! Good to see that you're still with the living!

For a minute there, Alisa and I thought that yer old ticker finally gave in."

"Like I told the lady earlier, I don't die that easily! Now get back to yer feet and start throwing lead at your old buddies!"

More bullets flew past them. Garrett and the others ducked and the bullets struck the ledge kicking up more dirt and pebbles at them.

"For a minute I forgot that we were in the middle of the fight for our lives here! You just interrupted me from a wonderful dream I was havin' about this lovely lady I met down in..."

Dixon's storytelling was cut abruptly by the sound of a gunshot. The shot sounded a lot closer than the others. Dixon even felt the heat from the bullet as it flew past him, coming a little too close for safety and comfort.

Garrett saw that one of the outlaws was climbing up the steep slope and had come much closer to them than his companions. Garrett didn't even think twice and acted. He pointed his revolver at the man and fired. Garrett moved so fast, it was almost unthinkable that he was on the verge of dying only moments earlier. The bullet struck the man right in the chest, and he tumbled down the slope back to the other outlaws. Garrett and the others heard the man scream as he fell to the ground.

The man landed back on the stony ground with a sick thud. Garrett and the others heard the outlaws shouting angrily at them from above. It was still a desperate situation, but Garrett allowed a smile to cross his lips.

"You'll pay for that! You'll all pay for that! Mikey was a good kid!"

They all recognized the angry voice that rose over the others as Claudio Henderson. Their prolonged stand had angered the outlaw leader. For him and his boys, this whole thing should never have gotten this far.

"We shoulda killed all of you at the camp back then! But nothin' you do is going to stop the inevitable! You all can't hide there forever, an' you're running out of lead to spray! Eventually me an' my boys are going to get up there, and when we do, you're all dead!"

A grim silence fell upon Garrett, Alisa and Dixon. They knew that Henderson's words echoed with the truth.

The heavy weight of that terrible reality weighed on them, until Garrett broke the silence.

"Yeah? Is that so? You talk a big talk conveniently hiding behind your men or a large boulder, Henderson! I've seen a lot of outlaws in my time! Taken down a good number of 'em too! You ain't nothin' special! You're nobody I ain't already seen before. You're just a two bit thug looking for some extra cash. Then when you get that cash, you blow it all on wine an' women in the same day! Why don't you come up here by yerself an' we can settle this up close an' personal?"

Garrett's spoke fighting words. They were the words of a desperate man and his companions with the odds stacked hopelessly against them. Despite that, the outlaws grumbled from the trees and boulders they hid behind. They held their fire, and for a moment, it seemed as if Garrett's words had actually hit them in a sensitive spot.

It was only after several tense moments that Henderson hammered his response from below them.

"Speaking of women and settling things up close an'

personal... why don't your lady friend come down here so me an' the boys can give her a little more of what she got before? We still got a lot where that came from, an' I'm sure she's just achin' for more! Hahaha!"

Henderson laughed like a rabid hyena, and his fellow outlaws all howled afterwards. Alisa heard everything including some catcalls and low whistles directed towards her. Her entire body trembled with rage and her face went red. She clutched at the rifle in her hands and was about to stand from where they were hiding and take a shot.

Garrett saw what was happening, and he tackled Alisa to the ground. Even if he was an old man, Alisa could still not wriggle herself free from his grip. She tried hard to extricate herself, but it was no use. Garrett could feel her struggling, and he only held her even tighter.

"What are ya doing? Let me go already! Let me go so I can take a shot at those scoundrels!" Alisa said.

"I ain't letting you go, Alisa! Don't you see? That's what they want! They want you to take a shot and break yer cover so they can put a bullet between yer eyes!"

"I don't always agree with the marshal but you have to listen to Garrett now, girl! He's right! Those skunks beneath us know what to say to make you angry enough to make a mistake. You make that mistake, an' it's the last one you'll ever make!" Dixon said.

Alisa knew that the two old men were right, but this knowledge did nothing to soothe the anger that was now boiling within her. Henderson's words only reminded her of what they did, and how dirty and violated she now felt. The feeling was powerful and overwhelming, and it would not easily be silenced. Perhaps it never would be silenced. This terrible reality dawned on Alisa, and she felt herself weakening and collapsing in Garrett's arms.

Garrett felt Alisa weakening. He could see how the life and energy seemed to suddenly be sucked out of her. Garrett felt Alisa go limp and suddenly tremble in his grip. She trembled and finally began to sob inconsolably. Garrett could do nothing but hold her even tighter.

"There now, girl. It's all right. It's all right. You go ahead an' cry it out. It's all right." he said.

Dixon saw Alisa collapse and give in to all her woes

and it enraged him. A fire was lit in the old outlaw, and he couldn't help himself. He exposed himself briefly from their cover and fired a single shot. It was wild, and none of the outlaws were clipped. Their answer was swift and hostile. Several shots were lined up and fired towards Dixon, but they were too late. The old outlaw had ducked and scooted back behind cover.

"Henderson! You an' your boys are nothing but a pack of rabid hyenas! Back when I led that gang of misfits it was different! Oh yeah, we robbed banks an' trains, maybe we even got a few innocents in the middle of our crossfires, but it was never like this! We would never have done anything that... that barbaric! We still had a code of honor! Alisa had nothing to do with any of this! You didn't need to violate her and satisfy your carnal urges!"

Henderson heard Dixon's impassioned pleas and his response was even more sarcastic laughter.

"You sure got a lotta nerve to speak about honor an' doin' the right thing! Why, you're the one that screwed us over with the money in the first place! If you didn't screw us over like that, we wouldn't have even been hunting for you all this time!"

Dixon heard the outlaw's words and he could only shake his head with silence and remorse. He knew that there was some truth to what he was saying.

"That dang no account's got a point! I should never have screwed over a bunch of skunks like that. But what's done is done an' we're here now. I should just go down there an' give myself up. They would surely leave you an' Alisa alone after that!" Dixon said.

Garrett shook his head. Even Alisa paused from her crying and gave Dixon a sharp look of disapproval.

"We all know better'n that, Dixon! If you go down there and give yourself up, it ain't going to change a thing! They ain't going to let us go easy. Not after we three killed some of their gang. No, you would just be giving yourself up for nothing. The moment you gave yourself up, they would resume shooting at me an' Alisa!"

"Gruff's right, Paolo! Surrendering to those demons won't change a thing! You might as well face it. The three of us are in this together, whether any of us likes it or not!"

It was hard for the old outlaw to hear what the old marshal and the young lady in waiting were saying because it was all true. Their words held much weight and only reminded him of the terrible situation they were in. A good part of the reason they were in this was because of his own scheming nature, and now they had little if any chance of coming through this alive. Whatever little chance they had of getting through this, was if they stuck together.

Dixon turned his glance towards the cave opening that was only a few feet from them. One of Alisa's whiskey bottles was empty. He had drunk the whole bottle earlier to try and cope with this terrible situation. His eyes spotted another bottle that Alisa had managed to bring up here with them. From where Paolo Dixon was, the whiskey bottle was very attractive.

"Gimme some more of that moonshine! I sure could use another good gulp of that stuff!"

"Enough of that already, Dixon! It was because of

your forked tongue that we found ourselves in this mess! If you hadn't double-crossed those buzzards down below us, they wouldn't be so hasty to come after us!" Garrett said.

Dixon was surprised at Garrett suddenly snapping like this. It had only been a few moments earlier that he had been stopping him from surrendering to his gang below.

"Is that so? Well, I had been warning you ever since you first picked me up that they were going to come after me! But you didn't listen did you? You and that stubborn old skull of yers didn't see reason to let me go, and let them catch me!"

"Stop it now, both of you! Ain't no good going to come out of you two arguing like two nannies! Come on Gruff, you were just saying earlier that there was no point in Paolo going down there and giving himself up. Ain't no point in arguing with him now." Alisa said.

Her words made sense and made the old lawdog take pause. He realized the futility of what they were doing and he backpedaled.

"You're right. Forget what I said. You ain't going to get no apology from me Dixon, but I ain't going to try and argue the point either. Ain't nothing more we can do now but try and somehow get through this, if we can."

Dixon took a deep breath and nodded. "I'm glad you saw some sense! Now can I take another swig of that moonshine, mother?" Dixon said with some sarcasm in his voice.

"I ain't your mother, and you can do whatever you please, Dixon. Go right ahead. Just don't go dozing off like that again. If we're going to make a stand here, we might as well make it wide awake."

"I won't doze off, Garrett. You can count on that. I just need a little distraction from all of this, is all."

"We all do. Might as well take a swig of that stuff myself." Garrett said.

"Let's all take a little of that stuff. Figure we might as well taste even a little satisfaction before we all go to wherever and whatever's out there." Alisa said.

"We ain't kicking up boot hill just yet, Alisa. And if we do go there, we're taking as many of those owl-hoots with us as we can. I'm still down for that.”

“I'll drink to that.”

It was Alisa who finally slipped out of Garrett's grip and reached for the whiskey bottle. She was careful to stay crouched and low as she crawled to get it. Garrett had the confidence in her, to let Alisa go and grab the bottle. She reached the bottle and crawled back with the two old men behind the rocky ridge that provided them cover. Not a single shot had been fired all this time.

“All right. Let's get some liquid courage down.” Alisa said.

Chapter Two: A Slim Chance

By the time Gruff, Alisa and Dixon had gulped down the moonshine, the day slowly began to give in to the night. In all that time there was still no gunfire exchanged from either side. A tense and momentary peace had fallen on both sides and both knew that the peace would only be momentary, at best. Despite this grim knowledge, both sides welcome the brief respite.

Below Gruff, Alisa and Dixon, the outlaws had lit a campfire. They could see the fires lighting the darkness and some sparks of light climbing up to where they were. The three exhausted companions could see some of the outlaws gathering around the fire.

"They're taking their time to fire at us. A lot of 'em are even sitting where they might be vulnerable to a shot or two." Alisa said.

"They're taking their time. They figure they got all the time in the world to come for us, considering they've got the advantage in numbers and in guns. Can't say I can argue that kind of reasoning too." Gruff said.

"Yoo hoo! Any of y'all cold n' tired tonight? Why

don't y'all come down with me an' my boys here where the fire's warm and friendly like? How about that whore you got there? She can come down and we can warm her up some more!"

It was the voice of Claudio Henderson that cut through the night. He called out to Gruff and his companions, but they all knew that he was not genuinely welcoming. None of them was going to take Henderson up on his invitation. They all knew he was just mocking them and goading them to make any mistake.

"Come on, girl I got some more right here for ya!"

"You might need some warm lovin' tonight we got more n' enough for ya!"

The other outlaws now began to heckle and throw insults from their camping ground. They were more than confident that they could handle anything that Gruff and the others might do. And why not? They easily outnumbered the three of them, and they had more than enough ammo to shoot them 20 times over. The outlaws were more than confident to throw insults at the three desperate individuals above them. None of them responded, not even Alisa, who seemed too exhausted to even care whatever insults Henderson or the other outlaws rained down.

"I should go down there, Gruff. You know it. I should go down there so I can give you an' especially poor Alisa there a fighting chance to survive this madness!"

It was Paolo Dixon. He continued to rant and bemoan their sorry situation through the night. Even as he did so, the outlaws continued to cackle and howl, but neither man paid them any attention. Alisa slept fitfully as both men kept watch.

"We already been through this earlier, Dixon. You go down there they will cut you to pieces without a second thought. After that, they will not hesitate to put both of us down after. It would be a pointless sacrifice."

"Would it really? We don't know that!"

"I'm getting tired of arguing with you, Paolo. If you really want to die, be my guest and slide on down there with them, if you want. Alisa's sleeping and I'm too tired to try an' stop you. But just remember, I warned you already."

Dixon remained silent as he pondered Gruff's words. The old marshal did have a point there.

"You know what, Gruff? Maybe you're right. Maybe I really don't want to go down there. If I really did want to go down there, I would have just made a break for it anytime. But I didn't. Instead, I'm here talking with you. Maybe I do speak with so many twists an' turns that even I don't know when I'm making sense!"

"Finally! You're starting to understand just how insufferable you can be! Maybe there's hope for you yet!"

"Come on, Garrett! I ain't so bad. I'm here fighting with you. Two old goats like us? We gotta stick together. It's like we talked about too. We're in this together, no matter what."

Garrett didn't answer Dixon and seemed preoccupied. It seemed as if something had caught his eye in the cave.

"What's wrong, old man? I don't like being ignored." Dixon said.

"Shut up! I think I spotted something. Something that might be important." Garrett said.

"What are you talking about?"

Garrett pointed towards the cave, but made sure he didn't extend his arm past the ledge. He didn't want his hand to get blown off while showing Dixon what he had noticed. "See that cavity to the left of the cave? It's just a few feet beside the cave! The stone ain't straight up. There's a large crack there, an opening! Can you see it?"

Dixon had to squint to notice it, but the shadows and light from the fire below illuminated the cavity that Garrett was talking about.

"Yeah, I can see it all right. And I think I know what you're thinking. Someone can climb up there."

"I think so, yeah. There might be some footholds to cling to, and it might be a real difficult climb, but I think it's possible."

"For the young lady there, maybe. But for old men like us? I'm not sure." Dixon said.

He hesitated, but Gruff's voice was firm and clear.

"You don't want to try an' climb up there, you're welcome to stay here until them boys of yours finally rush us, which could happen anytime."

Dixon paused. It would be a tough climb, but Garrett was right. It was still a lot better than waiting here for Henderson and his gang to overwhelm them.

Chapter Three: The Long Climb Up

Garrett and his trail companions waited until it was pretty late before they made their move. It was around 3am and very dark when they started to inch towards the cavity above the face of the cave. They all figured most of the outlaws would have given in to sleep by now, and there would only be one or two of them awake on watch. If they were lucky whoever was on watch might even be too drunk or sleepy to catch them making their move up the cave. Henderson and his gang made a ruckus the whole night and surely, they would be drained from all that.

Garrett, Dixon and Alisa began to move carefully and quietly, as they crawled under the ridge. They tried to minimize any sound as they crawled on their backs and on the ground. They also made sure not to poke their head or any other stray part of their anatomy over the ledge. Neither of them wanted any more stray bullets to come flying their way.

"So this is what a worm feels like." Dixon said.

"Quit jawing and keep crawling. You don't want 'em

to hear us and start firing!" Garrett whispered.

It was Alisa who made it first to the cave wall that led to the cavity. The light and shadows

from the campfire below gave her a fairly clear view of the rocky path up. There seemed to be rocky footholds and small cracks where one could get a good hold. Alisa took a deep breath as she turned to the two old men. They already knew what she was thinking.

"Go on and climb up first, Alisa! We'll follow once you're up on the other side." Garrett said.

Alisa nodded and slowly began to climb up. Her hands gripped the cracks on the rocky face, and her feet found some good footholds to move up. Alisa moved up pretty quickly and made good distance. Some small chunks of rock fell to the ground as she made her way to the cavity. Gruff and Dixon winced, as the rocks fell. They could only hope that the outlaws below were not seeing or hearing any of this.

Their spirits soared when they saw Alisa continue to clear the distance and climb up to the cavity. She continued to make good progress as she moved higher and higher towards the cavity.

"Better get a move on, Dixon. If a little lady like Alisa can do it, ain't no reason why an old "Speak for yerself, you old goat! And why should I go first? I can keep the rear while you climb first."

Dixon shook his head. "You go on ahead. I'll follow once you're up there. I'll keep an eye out for any of your boys." Garrett said.

Dixon wanted to argue and tell Garrett it would be better if he went first, but he decided against it. He could see the old marshal was not in any mood to debate the point. Dixon simply nodded and began climbing up towards the cavity.

"Fine. Just don't take yer time there and start climbing."

"I intend to do that."

Dixon didn't reply to Garrett. He continued to climb as Garrett watched over the outlaws' campsite. There was silence below only occasionally punctuated by the early morning breeze.

Garrett thought he was seeing things when he noticed that the sky was a dark crimson. He reminded himself that this was how it always was when the darkness was slowly giving up to the early morning's light. There were still several hours before sunrise, and Garrett couldn't help but wonder if he would live to see it. He brushed the thought away, not letting it settle in his head. Garrett was an old man, and one thing the years had taught him was that it was not good to dwell on thoughts like that, no matter how grim and imminent they seemed.

The old marshal thought that he saw movement below. He couldn't be sure, but it seemed as if some shadows danced in the light of the flames below. Could it be movement? Could the outlaws be making a move to climb up towards them? Garrett couldn't be sure.

"They could be making their way up here right now preparing to ambush us."

It wasn't a very pleasant thought, and it spurred Gruff to start climbing up towards the cavity, as well.

The old marshal threw caution to the wind and began to slowly climb up the cave wall. He couldn't be sure, but he thought he saw Dixon slipping a little as he climbed up. He couldn't see where Alisa was, as she had disappeared above them.

"Don't slip up now, Dixon!" Garrett said.

He saw Dixon move up higher, then hesitate. He saw his foot slip on some cracks and the old man began to slide down. Somehow, he managed to get ahold and continued to slowly move up. Alisa was much higher now, and seemed to be almost at the top.

"Come on, you old geezer! Get it together!" Garrett said.

He spoke as loud as he could without shouting.

Even with his soft voice, Dixon heard Garrett.

"I ain't a young 'un no more, an' it ain't an easy climb up!" Dixon said.

"You can keep complaining and wait til your friends get up the slope to welcome you with a lead party. Or you can keep climbing!" Garrett said.

Dixon didn't say anything and started to climb back up again. It was hard to argue with what he said.

Garrett glanced back down again. The slope was getting farther and farther away from them now. It was looking a little farther from where they were, and they had actually made good distance. That was the good news. The bad news was that Garrett thought he saw movement scurrying around the slope. He thought he caught sight of some shapes and shadows that were caught by the firelight. He could only assume that the outlaws were indeed slowly moving up the slope to try and ambush them. Their climb up the rock face of the cave was quite timely.

"Looks like we picked the right time to climb on out of here." Garrett muttered to himself.

He felt something tight in his chest, and his hands trembled. Garrett grit his teeth and cursed his misfortune. He knew exactly what this was, and it couldn't have come at a worse time. His heart was now starting to pound and protest the extra exertion of climbing up the cave's rock face.

Garrett thought he heard voices coming from the slope below them. He gritted his teeth and ignored the pounding in his chest, as he continued to climb.

Garrett blocked out the mounting pain and continued to move up. Even Dixon seemed to be moving at a deliberate pace up the rock face now.

Garrett heard the voices below him getting a little louder. Henderson's men were probably almost past the slope now. His hands grabbed any rocky purchase they could grip and the old marshal continued to soldier on. He could not hesitate now, and he did the only thing he could do. Garrett kept climbing up.

The sound of a gunshot made him pause. His hands and legs trembled as the shot cracked close to Garrett. He thought he would let go and tumble down just from the surprise of hearing the shot, but Garrett held on. The shot was wild and it missed him completely. The old marshal was grateful for that, but the fact that the shot was fired could only mean that the outlaws had probably scaled the slope by now.

Garrett kept moving up half expecting to be torn to shreds by lead as he was climbing up. He was surprised and relieved to see that no shots came to rip him to shreds. Garett found this curious, but he wasn't about to sit around waiting for the outlaws to get accurate.

As Garrett continued to climb unopposed, he realized what was happening. Henderson's men were firing into the cave and not straight up at the cavity. They hadn't realized that he, Dixon and Alisa had already made significant strides up the cavity. They had to make the most of this while they had the chance.

This brief respite wouldn't last. Garrett heard Henderson's men shouting below him, and they were a lot noisier and louder than usual. Two shots were fired again, and they came a lot closer to hitting Garrett.

"I think they've finally figured out what we're up to!" Dixon said.

"Forget about that and just keep climbing up! Don't stop for anything!" Garrett said.

"The old farts are up there climbing on the rock wall like a bunch of senile rats!" Henderson said.

His voice echoed through the caves and the outlaws responded. A hail of gunfire was shot towards the rock wall and a lot of the bullets flew close to Gruff. He felt several whizzed past him and hit the cave wall instead. Small bits of dirt and pebbles were chipped off by the gunfire. Gruff saw some pebbles detach and fall to the cave floor below. It was now easily at least twenty feet down. Garrett realized that if he or any of them fell from this height now, they would crack several bones in their body. If that happened, they would probably still be alive but be in excruciating pain. The outlaws would also be waiting just below like a pack of hungry wolves. Garrett and his trail partners would be lucky if they killed them off immediately. Knowing Henderson and his crew, they wouldn't do that. They had shown that they were not above inflicting pain and agony, like cats that played with dying rats before eating them.

"The blasted no accounts know we're here!" Dixon said.

"Forget that, shut up, and keep climbing! You're almost at the top of the cavity!" Garrett said.

"Yer making a lot of sense today, Garrett!"

Dixon looked up and saw the figure of Alisa leaning down from the top of the ridge. Garrett could see her now, as well. They both could see her round face and her kind eyes with a desperate look behind them. Alisa had managed to climb over the cavity and was now urging the two old men up.

"Gruff! Paolo! Come on up here! Hurry! You're almost there!" she said.

The two old men continued to climb up, urged on by Alisa's words. The outlaws below began to fire up towards them even more, their bullets angrily flying past the two old men.

Gruff could see that the outlaws were missing wildly. The cave was still pretty dark, and it was still some hours before sunrise. It was hard to get a good bead on the two old men as they climbed up the rock wall. Of course, Garrett and Dixon couldn't count on the outlaws having bad aim forever. This only spurred them to keep climbing up to the top of the cavity which was now so tantalizingly close.

Garrett could see and feel the bullets flying all around them. He decided they couldn't just keep climbing without some kind of response. He planted his feet firmly on the rocky purchase he was on. It was just wide enough for him to turn around. He did so and pulled out his revolver. Like the outlaws, Garrett couldn't really get a good shot out, with just the light of the campfire below. Still, he decided to just try and shoot at anything that moved. After all, there was a lot of movement beneath him.

Garrett fired a few shots down at the outlaws. He didn't hit anyone, but he did send them scurrying for cover. He provided some respite for Dixon and himself to keep climbing. Of course, the respite would be brief.

Garrett looked up and saw Dixon heave and lift himself up. He saw him tumble on the other side of the cavity. The old outlaw had climbed up to a safe spot behind the cavity. Now, it was Garrett's turn.

Garrett turned around and scrambled up to the top. He climbed as fast as he could, but the outlaws were now firing at him again. He could hear their angry and frustrated shouts beneath him. Gruff realized that these outlaws wanted them dead, real bad.

Henderson's men began to fire towards the old

marshal again. His ticker began to protest again but he ignored it. Garrett couldn't waste any time fretting about a bad heart, not now with gunfire erupting all around him.

"Just a little more you old scoundrel!"

"Come on, Gruff! You can do it!"

It was Alisa and Dixon. They were both leaning from the cavity and encouraging the old marshal to keep climbing. They were so close to him now, that he could almost reach him.

Garrett put his back to it, and almost sprinted to the top. Alisa and Dixon stretched out their hands for him to reach. Garrett saw it, and he reached for them.

The old marshal clutched Alisa and Dixon's hands and he held on tight. As he climbed up, he felt both the lady in waiting and the old outlaw pull him towards the other side. Garrett heard them both groan and grunt as they pulled him over. For a moment, he was flung upwards. The next instant he was on top of both of them, and they were on the rocky ground. They could hear the pops of the gunshots beneath them, but they were safely behind the cavity's ledge now. The bullets could not hit them.

"Well, I'll be. Not the most comfortable or graceful landing, but I ain't gonna complain." Garrett said.

"Get yer butt off of me already!" Dixon said.

"The important thing is, we're all still alive" Alisa said.

"Yep. That's true, but for how long we stay that way, is anyone's guess."

Chapter Four: Surprises

When the strange trio had gotten their bearings back, they all noticed a heavy and foul odor hanging in the air.

"Do you smell that?" Dixon said.

Alisa frowned and shook her head. "Yeah. It smells downright revolting. Like ten men decided to take a dump all at once."

"That's kind of what we're dealing with here unfortunately." Garrett said.

"What do you mean? Don't tell me some of Henderson's men got here before us and somehow want us to go back down because of the foul smell of their crap?" Alisa said.

Garrett shook his head. "If only it were that." he said.

"What do you mean? What could be worse than ten outlaws' poop?"

"The poop of a grizzly, that's what." Garrett spoke grimly as he pointed to the ground. Even though he was old his senses were still pretty sharp. He had already spotted the large dung heap a few feet in front of them.

His hand pointed towards the large brown pile. There were already several flies buzzing around it, and perhaps a few dung beetles would arrive. It was clearly the waste pile of a grizzly bear they were staring at. None of them were happy to see confirmation of the awful stench.

"Judging by the size of that dung pile, we might be dealing with a large grizzly." Dixon said.

"That ain't never good. Them large varmints are pretty good climbers. I guess it wasn't too difficult for the beast to climb up here."

Gruff and the others were just starting to ponder the possible presence of the grizzly when they heard angry shouts from below. They couldn't make out what the outlaws were saying as they were now so high above them. They could tell however, that they were angry and not pleased.

"Great. Right when we outsmarted those varmints, this has to happen now. How are we going to deal with a large and hungry grizzly?" Alisa said.

"We just have to stay alert. Hold on to your guns and move slowly. Keep your eyes an' ears open. Them grizzlies can sneak up on you when you least expect it." Garrett said.

The three of them began to move forward but very cautiously. The looming threat of the grizzly weighed heavily upon them as they walked.

"We've got to keep moving until we get to lower ground." Alisa said.

"Good idea. I just hope we don't have to go down a real steep slope. Dixon and I have been through a lot in the past couple of hours. I don't know if our brittle knees and legs could take the strain." Garrett said.

"Speak for yourself, old man! Perhaps you forget, but I am a master dancer in the art of Capoeira. I'm graceful and nimble and can land on both my feet any time!" Dixon said.

"Maybe when you were younger, Dixon. But you can't escape reality. You're as old as I am, maybe a little older. I doubt your legs could take such a steep descent."

Dixon didn't argue the point and just kept walking. The three of them walked for around a half hour or longer, passing by craggy rocks, pines and some bushes.

Garrett allowed himself to breathe a little easier. The ground seemed to descend gradually and at a manageable pace. He was relieved that the landscape seemed to descend more evenly and manageably. This would be good for him and Dixon and perhaps they could manage to get to lower ground without any incident.

A bloodcurdling sound cut through the air, and the three trail partners realized that this might just be a hope in vain.

"Did you hear that? It sounded like..."

"I heard it and I know what it sounded like Dixon. Ain't no one with a pair of ears coulda missed hearing it. That's the sound of an angry grizzly."

"Have any idea where the animal is?"

Garrett looked around. He spotted ferns, shrubs, and pine trees for as far and wide as he could see. There was no sign of the bear, and it was hard to gauge how near and far it was from the echo of its howl.

"Can't say for sure. But just by the sound of it, it might be close. It could be hiding anywhere in these woods. We'd best keep moving but just stay alert. Who knows when or where it'll jump out?

Dixon and Alisa were not reassured by Garrett's conclusion. It was enough motivation for them to just keep moving.

"I don't like this. I've never had to encounter a bear before." Alisa said.

"Consider yourself lucky. Believe me it ain't something you'll remember fondly." Dixon said.

"You had experience dealing with them?" Alisa said.

"Not me personally. I saw one of my trail partners get rushed down by one once. The thing just jumped out of the bushes an' mauled him. Despite its size you would be surprised. It moved so fast and hid so well behind the trees and bushes. The animal was built to surprise and ambush."

"What happened? You shot it?"

Dixon nodded. "Me an' the others, yeah. In the end the beast got drilled with lead all over its body for its trouble. But that poor guy it rushed? Well, he got his insides clawed out. Died a really long an' agonizing death."

"Both of you just quit yapping and stay alert! That bear could come at us anytime!"

They kept walking a little bit more and it was when the sun slowly started to rise when it happened. Gruff noticed something behind some thick and tall bushes. The shape was barely illuminated by the sunlight that was slowly breaking through the darkness.

Gruff carefully nudged Dixon as they kept walking.

"Do you see what I see? Over by those bushes. Some yards to my left."

Garrett motioned to the thickets in question. He tried not to make any sudden moves as he gestured towards it. He didn't want the bear hiding behind the bushes to get startled by any big moves like arms overextended or other sudden jerky movements.

"I think I can see it yes. The bruin is crouched deep in the bushes. I can barely make it out." Dixon said.

Garrett frowned. Dixon was right. The bear was crouched behind the bushes. Both of the old men knew that an animal like that crouched low if it was ready to pounce and attack.

"The sucker is getting ready to jump us. He could do it at any time!" Garrett said.

There was a low growl that came from the bushes. If there was any doubt that a bear was lying in wait ready to pounce on them, that sound dispelled any of it.

"You boys saw a bear?" Alisa said, with more than a hint of fear in her voice.

"I don't want to scare you Alisa, but there is a bear over there, and he's eyeing us good." Garrett said.

"I knew that low growl sounded a lot closer than I wanted it to be." Alisa said.

"Just stay calm and keep moving. I have an idea." Garrett said.

"What you got in mind?" Dixon said.

"I'm going to distract the thing. You take Alisa and keep moving. Don't stop for nothing."

Alisa and Dixon both heard Garrett and neither of them liked what they heard.

"What are you talking about, Garrett? You can't distract a bear like that! It looks hungry and ready to eat and kill at any time! A bear like that ain't going to fall for no distraction. It's just going to go straight for the nearest meal!"

"My thoughts exactly! If I can distract it well enough, it'll go for me not you and Alisa. Better I take the risk than either of you. Take care of her!"

"Gruff you can't be serious!" Alisa said.

Alisa glanced at Garrett and looked into his eyes. One look at his eyes and she knew that he was very serious indeed.

"Alisa, I ain't in no mood to argue this with you or Dixon. Both of you slowly but steadily keep moving forward. I'll keep that animal off of you."

"Paolo, he can't be serious! Don't let him..."

Dixon didn't even let Alisa finished. He pulled her with one hand and kept moving ahead. He knew his old rival well enough by now to see the futility of arguing with him. Paolo Dixon knew that the old marshal could be quite pig headed when he set his mind to it. When

Gruff Garrett had made his mind up, there was no convincing him otherwise, and this was one of those times.

"Come on, Alisa. Old Gruff wants to play the hero an' we don't have time to argue with him. Not with that big old bear just waiting to get its paws on its next meal."

Alisa still didn't like the idea of leaving the old marshal all alone to fend for himself against the bear. It just didn't seem like the right thing to do, especially after all they had been through. She wanted to protest, but Dixon and Garrett himself, were quite firm. With much regret, he found herself moving along with Dixon.

Garrett was glad to see Alisa moving out with Dixon. After all, she could be quite stubborn and headstrong. And Dixon also seemed to be showing more and more concern for Alisa and himself as the time went on.

"I never thought I'd see the day that Paolo Dixon actually developed a heart. Oh well, can't think about things like that. Best to keep my eyes and ears on..."

Garrett's musings were cut short by a loud howl. The howl was much louder and more pronounced than the other sounds the animal had previously made. It was clear that the bear was very serious now, and had only one thing in mind. It wanted to feed.

Gruff pointed his revolver at the bear and squeezed the trigger. A single shot rang out. Garrett didn't miss the bear, but the shot hardly bothered it. It only annoyed it. From where Garrett was standing, he probably could hit the bear, but a bear of that size was not going to be stopped by a single slug from a revolver.

"Hey, you stupid bruin! I'm here! Come fer me!" Garrett said.

He fired another shot at the bear again. For a moment, the bear stood on its hind legs and seemed annoyed by the shots from Garrett's revolver. It was at this moment that Garrett could see just how large the bear truly was. His eyes almost popped out of their sockets and his heart began to pound out of his chest. When the bear stood on its hind legs Garrett could see that it was much larger than he was.

"That's one large som-of-a-gun." Garrett whispered.

His tone was both fearful and respectful. Nature had

created a magnificent, yet terrifying predator and it was coming for him.

The bear fell on all fours again, and made a mad dash towards the old marshal. The enraged predator made a loud, guttural noise that echoed all through the bushes. It trampled several bushes and kicked up a large dust cloud as it charged towards Garrett. The old marshal was terrified, but he would not waver from his objective. He had gotten the bear's attention, and he was determined to keep it focused on him.

The bear rushed Garrett, and he was sure that the bear wasn't going to stop until it ate him. Garrett began to make a break for it. He ran as fast as his old and tired legs could carry him. Suddenly, Garrett was running with unusual speed, speed and energy he never knew he still had. It was truly incredible how the human body drew from unused reserves in times of extreme stress or life and death situations. This was one of them.

Garrett continued to run with the bear right behind him. He could hear the bear's strides as it ran on the rough ground. The ground underneath him literally shook as the large animal galloped closer and closer to the old lawman. Garrett figured he would probably die today, but at least he had bought time for Alisa and Dixon. As quickly as the thought popped up, the old marshal brushed it aside. He knew he was old, and he probably wouldn't survive this, but he didn't exactly savor the thought of being eaten alive by such a large and ferocious animal. Garrett had heard the stories about bears and bear attacks. He had heard about men who were slashed and thrown about, literally ripped from limb to limb by the animal. There were stories of men who literally saw their own innards ripped from their bodies before they died. He had also heard about men who were literally swimming in bear excrement and their own blood before they died. The horrible stories of bear attacks were numerous and could fill several nights worth of nightmares. Garrett didn't relish hearing about them, and he didn't relish experiencing them firsthand. He took a glance at his revolver. He figured he would leave one round for himself just in case the bear overwhelmed him. Garrett didn't want to go out in such a gruesome fashion.

Garrett continued to run but he could now hear the

bear snorting right behind him. He could almost smell the bear's foul breath and he could feel the heat from the bear's body as it was closing in. The terrible predator was almost upon Garrett now.

Garrett ran as fast as his old legs could carry him. A burst of speed kept him slightly ahead of the raging animal but only for a short time. At his age, there was no way Garrett could keep such a pace. It was either the bear caught up with him, or something unusual would happen. For the old marshal, it was the latter as he felt something on his foot. He couldn't be sure if it was some thick root sticking out of the ground, or a large rock. Whatever it was, he tripped on it, and it sent the old marshal sprawling flat on the ground.

Gruff went rolling on the ground, and the bear saw its chance. It charged right at the old marshal lying on the ground.

Gruff looked up and saw the large bear standing over him. It opened its mouth wide and growled. Garrett heard the bear bellow and its growl echoed all around. He thought his eardrums would shatter from the roar of the bear. Garrett could see saliva drooling from its long, sharp fangs. He could smell its hot breath coming upon his body. He could also feel the body heat radiating from the bear. It was like standing in front of the crater of a live volcano full of lava. The bear was more than eager to pounce on the old marshal now. The prospect of an easy meal was just too good to resist for the hungry predator.

"Well I guess I've lived long enough. A lot longer than most men. I got more than enough bullets left in the chamber an' it'll just take one to finish me off." Garrett said.

Garrett was about to end his life and his potential agony when the shot rang out. There was a sound like cracking thunder that echoed through the air. Garrett thought he saw a flash and some smoke from behind the bear. The bear also twitched as the shot rang out. It was struck from behind, and there was no way it could have avoided the shot. The shot struck the bear right at the back of its head. If the bullet had struck it on its body, perhaps it would have shrugged it off like some small annoyance. But the bullet struck fast and true in a vital area, ensuring the large animal's demise.

Garrett looked up and saw the bear's eyes widen with shock and surprise. It couldn't believe what had happened. It still couldn't accept it, but death had come. Garrett himself couldn't believe his good luck. He thought he was done for sure.

"What in tarnation?" he said.

Garrett's confusion was heightened even more, when he saw Alisa and Dixon running towards him. Both of them looked very relieved that he was still in one piece and breathing.

"Gruff! You're all right!" Alisa said.

"I'll say, you're one lucky old varmint! Your creaky, old hide's got more lives than a cat!" Dixon said.

Garrett looked around, just as incredulous to be alive. He saw a man standing across from him. The man held a smoking shotgun with both his hands. Garrett recognized the sound earlier as a gunshot from a shotgun. It was clear that this was the man that had shot the bear earlier. The man was dressed in furs and moccassins, the garb of trappers and mountain men. Beside him was an Indian woman. He also had a thick beard and eyes that looked quite strong and deliberate.

"I owe you my life Mister. You have my thanks. I'm US Marshal Gruff Garrett and these are my trail partners Alisa Pemberton and Paolo Dixon. And you're...?"

"Wayne Gainsboro at your service, sir. My wife Emilia."

The mountain man stretched his hand out and Garrett took it. Gainsboro helped pull the old marshal up and Garrett shook his hand. He wasn't surprised when he found that Gainsboro had a firm grip on his handshake.

"Nice to meet you, Mr. Gainsboro. If it weren't for you, I would have been that bear's lunch, and I wouldn't be talking right now."

Gainsboro smiled and shook his head. "Nice to meet you and your friends, Marshal. Don't mention it. Emilia and I were just passing through, doing our job. We heard that bear howling and roaring from a pretty far distance, and I knew that was our bear. We followed the sound of the bear here and well, I took the shot."

"Your bear? You and your wife were hunting for the bear?" Alisa asked.

Gainsboro nodded. "Indeed, Ma'am. I hunt for Twin Pines."

"Twin Pines?"

Gainsboro pointed some distance to the south. "A small town not far from here. Me and Emelia settled there, an' they pay me to hunt for food for them. I've had a lot of experience fur trapping back in the day and modesty aside, I think I can hunt pretty good."

"Ain't no doubt about that, Mr. Gainsboro. I'm still standing on account of your hunting skills."

"Please, call me Wayne."

"You can call me Gruff too."

Even as the men continued to discuss what had happened, Emilia had quietly moved towards the large bear. The once ferocious and dangerous beast was now lying deathly still on the ground. She took some knives and began to cut up the carcass.

"As you can see I shoot the critters big an' small an' the wife cuts 'em up. We get to feed some decent folk who pay us fer our troubles. It's a pretty decent trade-off if you ask me. Me an' my wife have been looking to take that bear down for some time now."

"Really? What's up about that bear?" Garrett said.

"The blasted thing dragged the headmaster of the school away and ate him alive."

For a moment, Garrett, Alisa and Dixon were silent. Gainsboro inadvertedly remided them of just how dangerous the bear was. It was sad to hear that a teacher would have met such a grisly fate.

"I'm sorry to hear about that." Alisa said.

"We all are. And hearing about it only makes me even more grateful for you saving my hash back there." Garrett said.

Wayne shook his head. "Like I said before, I'm just doing my job. I'm glad to have taken that bear down for you and our small community. It was already a great tragedy that the school headmaster was eaten alive like that. No one would want a repeat of that happening."

As they chatted Emelia took out her knives to prepare and skin the large bear. She was quite the silent type.

"Your wife... Is she Indian?" Dixon asked.

"Half actually. Her mother was taken by the Paiutes a long time ago, an' her father was a trapper like myself."

Wayne's story wasn't really surprising considering it was a common practice for Indian tribes to kidnap settlers and have children with them. Such practices would seem cruel and even barbaric as time went by, but they were the norm back in the day.

Garrett looked ahead to where Wayne was pointing. He could make out the small town of Twin Pines from where he was standing. It was a small settlement of tents, shacks and a few establishments. It wasn't far from where they were.

"I can see your town from here, Wayne. Ain't got no lawman there, I reckon?"

Wayne shook his head. "It's a small an' sleepy town as you can see. The folk there are pretty peaceful and generally keep to themselves. We've never really seen the need for a lawman these past few years. I'm probably one of the few people around who know how to use a piece."

"Interesting. Sounds like a nice little place. Me an'

my friends could use a short break from all our traveling." Garrett said.

Gainsboro nodded and smiled good-naturedly. He seemed like a very welcoming and disarming fellow.

"There's a bath house and a saloon down there along with a small boarding house. Nothing fancy, but I'm sure you good folks could sure use some R n R."

"Oh you bet we could! I'm so tired I could just collapse on a soft mattress." Alisa said.

"Sounds really inviting. The walk ain't so far from here. If you don't mind me an' my friends will check it out." Garrett said.

"Be my guest. Emilia and I will prepare the carcass and be down there in a bit."

Garrett, Dixon and Alisa began the trek to Twin Pines. It was a short and pleasant walk as the slope descended evenly, and the threat of any predator had been effectively taken care of by Wayne.

Dixon shook his head. "I can't believe an old outlaw myself is saying this, but I actually feel bad that there ain't no lawman around yonder parts. Might have helped us with our little situation back there.

"I ain't surprised there's no sheriff down there. Small towns like that usually don't have one. It's probably not even on most maps." Garrett said.

"So we ain't going to get no help for our little problem back there? Ain't no one there coming to back us up against those no accounts." Alisa said.

"Wayne looks quite competent with guns. I reckon he could probably take out some of those outlaws if it came down to it. But I don't want to drag him or the town into our mess. I'm not even sure he would be willing to help take your gang out." Garrett said.

Dixon frowned and scowled at Garrett. "My gang? They were trying to kill me just like they were trying to kill you an' Alisa back there. They ain't my gang no more!"

"An outlaw like yourself hardly if ever changes."

Dixon was genuinely offended by Garrett's words now.

"What are you trying to insinuate? You saw how I put neck out on the line for you back there! You ain't got no right to doubt my sincerity, Gruff!"

"Will you two little girls stop jawboning already? I'm too tired to endure you two old men pulling at each other's hair! We all still got a problem that we just put aside for the moment, and that's Henderson and his men. The only chance we have of getting through that problem is if we work together. Ain't no room for any of us to argue an' fight."

Upon hearing Alisa's words, the two old men backed off. They could both see the wisdom in what she was saying and grudgingly dropped their argument. They walked towards the small town of Twin Pines without any incident.

Along the way, they came upon some young boys running outside town. The boys looked quite excited as they ran around.

"Did you folks hear that? There were shots fired outside a' town!"

"Did Mr. Gainsboro shoot the big old bear that ate

Mr. Kendal?"

The boys just walked up to Garrett and the others with no hesitation and asked away. Even Garrett and Dixon who had been arguing earlier couldn't help but smile when they noticed the eager and trusting nature of the young boys.

"If Mr. Kendal is the school headmaster well yeah, Mr. Gainsboro did shoot the bear earlier." Garrett said.

"Did you see him shoot the bear, Mister?" one of the boys asked.

Garrett bent over and smiled at the little boy. "I sure did. I even almost got eaten by the bear myself! But Wayne was right there to shoot the bear in the back of the head before it got me." he said.

The two boys' eyes widened and their jaws dropped. Just the idea of getting up close to the bear without getting eaten was the most thrilling thing ever for them.

"Really, Mister? You survived a genuine bear attack? That's incredible! Was the grizzly huge?"

"Yeah! And did it manage to scratch you or

anything?"

Garrett chuckled. The sheer innocence and enthusiasm of the little boys were infectious. They reminded Garrett and Dixon of something they may have lost so long ago.

"Lemme tell you boys, if that bear even nicked me, I might not be here standing with you to tell the tale. It was definitely one dangerous and ornery fellow. I sure wouldn't want to encounter another bear for the few years I got left!"

"Why not, mister? Them bears can't be so bad! I'm sure once I learn how to handle a six-shooter, I'll shoot a whole lotta 'em in between their eyes! Why I'll skin a lot of 'em alive an' make a good living hunting them down like Mr. Gainsboro!"

Garrett, Dixon and Alisa couldn't help but chuckle at the young boy's bravado. He was clearly unaware of the harsh realities of life and was still quite young and innocent. His companion was just a little more aware of the harsh realities of life.

"Come on, cut 'em a little slack, Toby! Can't you see

the man's an old timer already! Ain't no way an old timer can stand up to an angry grizzly!"

"Ain't no way you're going to catch me getting that old and weak, no way! When I grow up, I'll be even stronger than Mr. Gainsboro! They'll all know who I am when I grow up!"

Gruff, Dixon and Alisa couldn't help but smile at young Toby. He was definitely very confident and sure of himself. Gruff and Dixon looked at each other, and neither didn't have to say a word. They both agreed silently with each other. They were both old men, and they couldn't help but wonder how long Toby would remain so confident and sure of himself. Surely, the years would chip away at his confidence leaving him as old, tired and broken as they were. Old men like themselves had learned to accept this inevitable reality.

"I'm sure they will Toby. I'm sure they will." Gruff said.

Dixon nodded and smiled with approval. Garrett and Dixon shared the same sentiment. Both of them were well aware of the little boy's likely fate. The two old men had seen their fair share of misery between them, but that was no reason to dampen the boy's spirit. And at the back of their minds and hearts they both held on to the slightest hope. Maybe, just maybe this boy would actually make a difference in his life when he got older.

"Them some hot springs there yonder?" Dixon said.

He noticed some hot springs just above the small town. From where they were, Garrett also noticed the natural water vapor rising from the water.

"Sure would be nice to get a nice warm bath to rest these old, weary bones." Garrett said.

"Mr. Ward runs the local bath house! Y' all can get a decent warm bath there for $2 each." Toby said.

"I think I would like that proposition all right. That sounds well an' mighty fine, indeed." Garrett said.

"I gotta agree with Gruff, there. I wouldn't mind soaking my own scrawny bag of bones in a hot tub for some time." Dixon said.

"You two can enjoy your bath. Me? I think I'd like to lie down and get some rest somewhere." Alisa said.

"You can rent a room at the Inn in town, lady!"

"Thank you for that, boys. I think I'll do just that, while my friends have their bath."

"Well, me an' Francis here had best take our leave. We want to see Emelia skin that bear good!"

Francis and Drake ran off to where Wayne and Emelia were. Garrett and his two companions were almost at Twin Pines now.

"You boys go on ahead and check that bath house there. I just need to check into a room and get some shuteye at the inn." Alisa said.

"Some shuteye wouldn't be a bad thing for any of us. I'm so tired and I can't believe we're all still alive after everything we've been through." Dixon said.

Once they entered the town, they dropped Alisa off at the inn, before heading off to the bath house. The town was quite small and quaint. Only a few small houses dotted the area, but it did have just about everything a town would need to manage. Aside from the inn and bath house, Garrett and Dixon spotted the town's only saloon, as well as the school and a small chapel.

"Looks like a quiet enough place. Would have been nice to settle down in a small town like this." Garrett said.

"Maybe in another reality, Garrett. Old men like us don't have it in us, to settle down."

Garrett didn't answer Dixon. Perhaps he was right. It was a thought that bothered Garrett but he didn't say it.

A short walk later, the two old men finally made it to the bath house. It was nothing more than a small tent with four bathtubs. There was an old pack mule that stood at the front of the tent with some pails on its sides. No doubt, this was how they transferred water from the springs to the bath house. Right in front of the tent was a sleeping man that was just as old as Garrett and Dixon. A large brown dog lay beside the seated and dozing old man. The dog was sleeping but jumped wide awake as Garrett and Dixon approached.

When the brown dog sprang into action, it stood up, wide awake and ready for action. When it stood on all fours, it revealed itself to be a much larger dog than it appeared. The dog was large but thin and lanky. It had long legs and a robust frame. Despite its thin frame, the dog looked quite fast and powerful. Its bark was also full and loud.

The dog's barking started Garrett, Dixon and its owner. The old man woke up with a start.

"What going on?" he said.

"You oughtta leash that dog of yours! A dog that big could bite someone hard!" Dixon said.

"Dixon's right! He don't look real friendly-like!" Garrett said.

The old man shook his head and motioned towards his dog. When the large dog saw his

master stand up and move towards him, his demeanor changed abruptly. It suddenly crouched and hunched on all fours. It was clearly ashamed and now timid and submissive in its posture. It was almost comical to see such a large dog take such pains to make itself look smaller and less threatening.

"Sorry good sirs! Geras here ain't a nasty feller. He just really looks the part. He's scary an' all, but his bark is definitely worse n' his bite. Don Ward at yer service."

Geras whined after his owner spoke to emphasize the point.

Garrett shrugged his shoulders. "I guess so. Well, me an' my friend here would like to use your bathtubs, Mr. Ward." Garrett said.

"Why you actually called me a 'friend' Gruff!

I do believe you're finally havin' a change of heart!" Dixon said.

Garrett glared at Dixon. "Don't push it, Dixon."

"Sure. I got two bathtubs available here." Ward said.

"Reserve one more tub for another friend of ours." Garrett said.

Ward smiled at Garrett. "As long as you got the six dollars for it, I'll reserve the tubs."

Garrett handed Ward the six dollars. The old man smiled as he took the money.

"You two gents can strip and settle down for a moment while I prepare the hot water. It's a short ride from here to the hot springs. I won't be long. You two just sit tight and make yourselves comfortable." Ward said.

Ward got on the pack mule and the animal groaned. For a moment, Gruff and Dixon were worried that the animal might collapse from the old man's weight. The pack mule didn't seem that old, but it did seem quite weary from all its tasks. Somehow, it held its portly master and its buckets and began a slow, but deliberate trek to the hot springs which was just a short distance. It ambled away and Geras trotted along with it for a while before returning to the tent and settling down beside the two tired, old men.

"I hope that dog don't suddenly charge at us and bite." Dixon said.

Garrett shook his head. "Nah. Ward said his dog's friendly, and I've seen this kinda dog before. It's just a little skittish, but this kinda dog don't really want to bite or cause any trouble. It's used to people hanging around here by now."

"I guess so. I'll take your word for it. Somehow, you've actually managed to survive this long and even protect me and Alisa from those double-crossing owl-hoots. That ain't easy fer sure, so I know, you know what yer talkin' about." Dixon said.

Garrett frowned. "I was protecting Alisa from them. You're just a bonus."

Dixon chuckled. He didn't seem affected by Garrett's disapproving look.

"You like to frown an' act tough all the time Garrett, but you can't fool me no more. I know you a lot better now. Deep down beneath all that tough swagger, yer just a sweet an' cuddly teddy bear is all."

Garrett shook his head and changed the topic, pretending not to hear what Dixon said.

"You think they'll make it back here? That poor mule looks as old and tired as we do." Dixon said.

"I reckon they will. The town is the epitome of sleepy and off the beaten path. A place like this ain't seen any trouble at all. That mule has probably lived a better life than we have." Garrett said.

"You think so, eh? An' speakin' of trouble, you think Henderson and his boys will find us here?"

"Doubtful. This place is some distance from the top of that cave. And I figure they'd have a hard time tracking us down. I made sure to cover our tracks back there just to be sure. And that's even assuming they all manage to climb up to the top of that cavity. Lookin' back in hindsight, that was a mighty crazy thing we managed to do back there. That was easily around a 30 foot climb to the top. I can't believe a pair of old fogeys like us managed to climb up to the top like that."

Dixon shrugged his shoulders. "Just like you to cover our tracks eh, Garrett? You're always one to prepare for every situation. I've always known you to be very meticulous. And about how we managed to climb out of that cave back there? Well, we were desperate. You, of all people should know how desperation can spur a man to do near-impossible things." he said.

Garrett and Dixon began stripping down to their long underwear. This was the first genuine moment that either man had a chance to settle down, relax and catch their breaths. It was only now that they both noticed just how awful they looked and smelled. The stench of the trail was heavy on both men and their clothes.

Garrett looked down and noticed there were several cuts and blisters on his bare feet. There

were also callouses that were starting to form in some areas. Some of the hardened skin might have been painful, but Garrett had been too busy running for his life to notice.

Dixon didn't fare any better. While he didn't have as many blisters and callouses on his feet, his body was bruised and battered. There were several bruises and welts on his back and there was a swelling on the back of his head from being pistol whipped.

"I can't believe we look this bad. Takes a moment like this for things to slow down to make you realize how much you need to just take a rest. I hope they got some cleaners who can clean our clothes or something. We should have asked." Garrett said.

"I reckon they probably do. We can ask Don when he comes back."

It didn't take long for Don Ward to return. The mule seemed to struggle with every step, as it now carried Ward and the buckets of hot water from the springs.

Geras barked and howled his approval at the return of his master.

"Howdy boys! Miss me? Heh, told you I wouldn't take long. Now if you'll excuse me, I just need to get this water to the tubs."

Ward got off the mule and carried two bucketfuls of the hot water. He moved them to the bathtubs with surprising speed and balance. Geras chased Ward around but kept a respectful distance from Ward, making sure he didn't bump into him. It was clear he was used to this kind of work.

It didn't take long for Ward to pour all the hot water from the springs into the tubs.

"Well gentlemen, y'all enjoy and relax. The hot tubs are ready for you to soak your weary bones in. I'll prepare another tub when your friend arrives." Ward said.

"You do that. She's Alisa Pemberton, a fetching young lady. A lot younger than us weary old men for sure." Dixon said.

"Heh! I'll be sure to do that, sirs! Just relax and enjoy yerselves. You deserve a break from yer weary travels.

Here, have some soap and brushes."

Ward handed the two men 2 bars of soap, and 2 brushes for their bodies. Garrett and Dixon took the toiletries and proceeded inside the tent.

Once inside the tent, Garrett and Dixon promptly stripped down to their birthday suits and settled into the bathtubs with hot water. The water wasn't even hot. The temperature was just right to soothe their weary bodies.

"Ah, does that feel good or what?" Dixon said.

Garrett couldn't argue with Dixon. Both of the old took the time to take a deep breath and soak their tired weary bodies in the warm water of the tubs.

The water felt good on Garrett's body, soothing and refreshing him. He took several deep breaths and for the first time in a long while, he didn't feel his heart pounding out of his chest. It was quite the wonderful and invigorating feeling.

"Boy did I need this." Garrett said.

"Both you and I."

The two old men had to pause for a bit and simply

savor the moment. Both Garrett and Dixon had gotten so used to shooting at someone, or getting shot at, that gunfighting and danger had almost become routine. The two old men had lived out their long lives with mostly danger and death as their common companions. They had simply forgotten what it was like to just sit back and enjoy a quiet moment like this. It was almost surreal for both men, especially considering these peaceful moments were spent with each other, two men who at one time, were sworn enemies.

"You know my old ticker ain't complaining right now. I don't feel like some giant crab's crawling on it, or that it might just burst right outta my chest." Garrett said.

"I think I know what you mean. I've gotten so used to the sound of gunfire ringing in my ears. Now, all I hear is just the wind an' a cool breeze blowing. The silence is almost deafening." Dixon said.

"I could almost get used to this. Almost." Garrett said.

"Like ah said before, I know you all too well by now Garrett. An old lawdog like yerself ain't one to quit or retire. A man like you lives an' dies by the gun upholding his law. I ain't got nuthin' against that, believe me. I even kinda respect it actually."

"Is that so?"

Dixon nodded solemnly. "Of course. From one man to another, I respect someone who has values an' sticks to 'em. For one thing, I know that when all this is said an' done, you're still going to take me in. You're still going to haul my butt to prison just like your superiors want you to do. You still want to finish your last job, of course. And I know I can't convince you otherwise. I'm resigned to my fate."

"That's where you're wrong, Dixon. From this day on, you're a free man."

Dixon couldn't believe what he heard. Garrett sounded very serious, but Dixon still thought he had to be joking.

"Aw come on, Gruff! Don't rub me like that. An slimy outlaw like myself might actually believe what you're saying and get disappointed when you eventually cuff me."

Garrett shook his head. "Don't want to believe me, that's fine. But I already told you and you can take my word for it. You're free to go. As far as me an' the government is concerned, taking you to prison is just too much of a hassle. I ain't going to bother with it, no more. You ask me, I got bigger fish to catch now."

Dixon's eyes widened and his jaw dropped. "Lord almighty, you are serious, ain't ya? You're really going to let me go. Ah kin see it in yer eyes and hear it from the sound of yer voice. You really don't care about taking me in no more."

"I meant every word I said, Dixon. It's just too much of a hassle to even bother taking you in now. Especially with your boys running loose like this."

"Fer the last time Gruff, they ain't my boys! I am not associated with those barbarians. Not anymore, at least."

"Whatever. Well, after what they did to Alisa, an' all the things they've done, I intend to make 'em pay for it. Pay for all of it. I figure it;s the only decent thing an old lawman like myself can do now. You just take Alisa and the two of you just run away from here as fast as you can.

You don't want to be in the middle of all the shooting when it happens."

Dixon knew that Garrett was serious now, and he didn't like a word that the old marshal was spouting from his lips.

"Are you out of your senile mind? Have you really lost it old man? Last time I checked they outnumber you..."

"I know how to count, Dixon! I've lived long enough to not fear death no more. Ain't no one gets through this life alive, anyway! If I'm going to go down, I might as well take down as many of those blasted rats to hell with me!"

"Very heroic and very stubborn of you, Garrett. I am honestly not surprised! But I'll let you know this ain't like the incident with the bear no more. Once Alisa hears about this, there ain't no shaking her off, or me for that matter! We ain't just going to let you run off alone to get yourself killed. This thing is all of our problem now. We're all in this together whether you like it or not."

Garrett could tell from the way he was speaking that

Dixon was just as serious as he was.

"You know it's your death sentence if we all see this through til the end, Dixon. But old men like us have lived long enough. It wouldn't really matter if we died now. We've both lived long enough. But Alisa, that's another story. She's young, an' she's still got her entire life ahead of her. I wouldn't want her dying, taken out by an outlaw's stray bullet."

"You think I don't have a heart too? I don't want nuthin' happenin' to Alisa either, Garrett. But she's been with us from the start. There were many times that stray bullet could have hit her, but she somehow survived. There ain't no guarantees in this or anything, but Alisa's a grown woman. Ain't no way you can force her not to go with you, if she insists on going. And we both know she will."

Garrett remained silent. He knew the old outlaw was right. Alisa was quite a stubborn young lady. When her mind was made up, it was almost impossible to stop her from doing anything. Garrett knew he wouldn't be able to convince her not to see this whole thing through, but he couldn't live with himself if she died. He had already endured the death of Katie Kemp. That was terrible for Gruff and the whole reason he took on this assignment, that had become much bigger now. He wouldn't allow Alisa to die. With Katie, Garrett had seen enough innocents die.

Garrett and Dixon remained silent for the remainder of their baths. Both men pondered what the future held, but they were both pretty sure that a lot of danger was in store for them.

When they were done bathing, they dressed and thanked Ward for the baths.

"Thank you for the use of your baths, Mr. Ward." Garrett said.

"Indeed. The baths were truly refreshing. Just what we both needed." Dixon said.

"I was happy to help. And thank you both for your payment. Like you said, I'll keep one bathtub reserved for your friend, Alisa. Oh, and by the way! You people have passed by our town at the perfect time! I heard that our local hunter Wayne Gainsboro finally killed that big man-eating bear that ate the school headmaster! Heard the shots from way over here too. Must have been a real shootout!"

Garrett nodded and smiled. "We both are very aware of the fact. Mr. Gainsboro actually saved me from the bear himself. The bear was about to pounce on me, when he arrived in the nick of time. He shot the large animal behind its head, just before it was about to well, you know."

Don 's eyes widened with genuine surprise and amazement.

"Is that so? Gee, golly! That is just incredible! You are indeed a fortunate man, Mr. Garrett. All the more reason you and your friends should head on down to the saloon later tonight. I heard there's going to be a big celebration there, for Wayne's success. I'm sure there'll be lots of whiskey on the house!" he said.

Garrett chuckled and shook his head. "I think we'll pass, Mr. Ward. Old men like us need our sleep. We ain't young anymore an..."

"Oh you can speak for yourself, Garrett! I would love

a good drink an' I ain't about to pass such a fine opportunity!" Dixon said.

"Heh. Well, I ain't going to stop my friend here from partaking of your local hospitality. You know where we could get a good meal? I think I can now speak for myself and Dixon when I say that we're both pretty famished."

"Head on down to the inn. You can't miss it from here. Mrs. Kendall cooks wonderful meals there an' I'm sure she can fill your bellies up in no time."

"That's where Alisa checked in earlier. Come on Gruff. Let's get ourselves some grub."

Garrett smiled and shook Ward's hand. "We'll be heading there now. Thanks for the bath again, Mr. Mead."

"Anytime, Mr. Garrett."

It was a short walk to the inn, but when they arrived there, Garrett and Dixon immediately noticed the difference between Don Ward and Maude Kendall.

Garrett knocked on the front door of the inn, and a

large, portly woman opened the door.

"Good day, Ma'am. We would like to get a meal and have some food to eat. We're willing to pay and..."

"Good day. Now I wonder what rock did you two old boys crawl out of?" the woman said.

"We've just been traveling for some time, and we're pretty tired and hungry is all." Dixon said.

He was surprisingly patient and polite with the portly and grumpy woman.

"Take a seat there. I'll get the menu. We have two vacant rooms. Don't dirty them too much. I just cleaned the bedsheets myself."

When they sat at the table, and the woman left them alone, Dixon whispered to Garrett. "That must be Mrs. Kendall. She's quite the friendly and hospitable host, isn't she?"

Garrett chuckled. "I'll say."

Unlike Ward, who was clearly cheerful and outgoing, Kendall was very grumpy and irritable. The moment she met Garrett and Dixon she was very unwelcoming. She did however, accept their payment. She allowed them to come in and have a meal. After all, she was still not one to push away any potential customers.

"Here. We've got some beef strips, some stew, and some steamed beans and steak."

Mrs. Kendall frowned as she tossed the menus to Garrett and Dixon. She seemed almost aghast to be serving these three strange and unkempt old men in her dining room.

"We'll have two steaks and some whiskey. What do you say, Dixon?"

"I would like the taste of some fresh meat on my lips all right. You might as well toss in two sticks of cigarettes while you're at it." Dixon said.

"So it's settled. We'll have two steaks and a bottle of your finest whiskey and two cigarettes. We'll also have one extra steak delivered to Alisa Pemberton. I do believe she checked into your fine establishment a few hours ago." Garrett said.

"She did. And quite a fine young lady indeed. Just looked a little worn and strained from riding the trails."

Mrs. Kendall frowned after speaking, as if the strained act of courtesy was a genuinely difficult thing to do.

"Poor girl must have really been tired from all that excitement." Garrett said.

Mrs. Kendall turned from the two old men and spoke much softer, hoping they would not hear her.

"I wonder what kind of "excitement" she had with two old vultures like yourselves." she

hispered.

Garrett chuckled as Mrs. Kendall left. "I heard that." he said.

He didn't say it any louder. He wasn't in any mood to argue with Mrs. Kendall or start a scene. He just found it a little amusing that she frowned on their presence at the inn.

"I heard what that portly lady said too, Gruff. What's her problem?" Dixon said.

"I think we both know that people like that carry a heavy chip on their shoulders all the time."

"What would be bothering someone like her?"

Garrett shrugged his shoulders. "Who knows? Maybe someone like her had dreams once. Dreams of leaving this small town for bigger things. Dreams that just never happened. Or it could be a plethora of other things. If there's one thing I've learned in this life, it's that people are pretty complex creatures. They're always pretty surprising. I mean just take a look at us, fer instance. Who would have thought two frail, old men like us would have such sharp senses honed by so much violence in our lives?"

Dixon nodded. "Good point. I guess men like you an' me, we gotta have sharp eyes an' ears. Gotta be ready for any kind of threat, I reckon." Dixon said.

"Exactly, Dixon. You an' me just can't stop bein' alert, I guess. We're like that poor grizzly that Gainsboro shot earlier. Always alert an' ready for anything. Makes it hard to relax an' all."

"Exactly. Only made that bath earlier even more enjoyable. I reckon that was the first time in a really long time either of us had a chance to just sit back an' relax."

"Well, we can still relax right now, I reckon. We might as well enjoy the moment while it's here."

Dixon whistled low and smiled. "A quiet moment with a man who was once my deadliest enemy. Lord almighty. Will thy wonders ever cease eh, Gruff?"

For the first time in the whole time they were together, Gruff smiled at Dixon. The old outlaw was genuinely surprised to see the old marshal smile and reveal his surprisingly pearly white teeth. Or at least most of his teeth were white. There were still some yellow ones between the edges, but having mostly white teeth was a genuine miracle in those days.

"Heh. I guess them wonders don't ever cease all right." Garrett said.

"An' speaking of wonders, I reckon this is the first time you've ever smiled and shared a light moment with me, this entire trip Garrett. Maybe you are getting soft on me. Maybe I'm starting to grow on you." Dixon said.

"You're really pushing it Dixon, you know?"

Mrs. Kendall returned with two plates of freshly cooked steaks and a bottle of whiskey.

"There you go boys. Enjoy. And I'm perfectly happy where I am, thank you."

Garrett and Dixon almost jumped up when they heard Mrs. Kendall's response. Neither of them could say anything or wanted to. It would be hard to argue with someone like her, and neither man was inclined to exert the effort.

"Like I said before, people are always surprising." Garrett said.

"I'll drink to that!"

The two men drank the whiskey and gobbled up the steak. It was the best meal both men had in a long while. When they were done, they enjoyed a good smoke to let it all down.

Chapter Five: The Nightmare

Tonight, the lights and sounds from the small saloon at Twin Pines were much brighter and louder than usual. Even the smell of cheap cigarettes and booze was a lot stronger from the establishment. The piano player played the piano a little louder than usual, and the men inside were a lot more festive and rowdier. The whole mood from the saloon was infectious and it almost seemed as if the entire town was headed to the saloon, and for good reason.

The celebration was spilling out from the saloon and into the whole town. Men and women were dancing on the streets leading to the saloon. Most of the men in town found themselves drawn to the saloon like Dixon, for the free drinks and a chance to gamble their money away. The whole mood in the small town was festive and upbeat. Everyone was happy that the large grizzly that had eaten the schoolmaster was finally put down.

Paolo Dixon wasn't fully sure how he managed to get to Twin Pine's local saloon. He seemed to have been drawn by the noise and the lights of the saloon like a moth to a flame. This wasn't surprising. After all, Dixon was always one to celebrate and get a drink, whenever he had the chance.

"That was one dangerous bear. I'm glad it's finally been put outta its misery. We didn't need a predator like that making our lives even harder than it already is!"

"Agreed! I'm glad Gainsboro put that thing down! I knew headmaster Rollins. He was a good man. He was my teacher, an' my kids' teacher before that bear ate him alive."

"Agreed! The town lost a good man in Rollins, but we're pretty lucky to have Gainsboro around to take care of problems like that bear an' hunt for us!"

Inside the saloon, talk of Wayne Gainsboro and how he killed the bear dominated the conversation. The trapper was already a prominent figure in town but with this one kill, he became even more of a huge figure in town.

"Ah'm so glad you came at the right time when you did, Mister Gainsboro. You saved my friend. I'll drink to that!"

Dixon raised his glass and clinked it with another glass. Gainsboro smiled at Dixon and the two of them took another drink of whiskey.

"Thank you for the kind words, Mr. Dixon. I just do my best here. I'm really glad to be appreciated like this."

"Ah, you're too modest, young man! The work you do here is essential fer yer small town. I don't see none of these men goin' around hunting man-eating bears."

Gainsboro shook his head. "I can't really ask anyone to do what I do, Mr. Dixon. Everyone's got a role to do in this town. It's just that ain't none of them have that role of hunting or taking down wild animals. I'm the only one who can do what I do. And I just I gotta do it well for everyone's sake."

Dixon took another swig from the whiskey. He had long lost count how many glasses of whiskey he had drank today. Dixon's head was spinning and he was starting to rant. He wasn't thinking straight, but he didn't really mind. It was more than a nice feeling and Dixon savored it.

"Ah, you're truly a humble kid, ain't ya? Ah sure wish I was as humble as you back when I was just as young. Ah, I was once as young as you were you know... I was just as strong as you, and maybe better with a gun. I could have taken that bear out with a gun too!"

Dixon continued to drone on, not fully aware of what he was saying. He thought he noticed Gainsboro nodding and smiling as he continued to speak. Gainsboro wasn't saying much now, and Dixon seemed to just be talking on and on, with no end in sight.

"Bears are a menace to every well-minded settler round these parts! I tell ya, I have no idea why God would even create such beasts. All they ever wanna do is eat and take a poop. That's all they ever wanna do. Ain't none of them ever done an honest day's work if you ask me. A lotta of 'em are just like the boys I used to ride with. Treacherous and quick to ambush ya when they have the chance!"

"That's a whole mouthful coming from a back stabbing snake like yerself! We weren't the ones who hid the money!"

Dixon turned around with shock and surprise. He recognized that voice all too well. He just didn't expect to hear it in this small town so soon. Dixon turned around and saw Claudio Henderson standing in front of him.

"Henderson! What are you doing here? And how did you find me?" Dixon asked.

Henderson glared at Dixon and smiled at him. There was no warmth or friendship in his smile. It was the smile of a cat that had backed a tiny mouse to the corner. Henderson felt the same rush of excitement as the cat would, and now he was also about to pounce on his prey. And just like the cat, he wasn't about to devour Dixon just yet. No, he wanted to savor the moment and toy with him.

"It wasn't really difficult considering how long I've been doing this. You shouldn't be surprised, Dixon. Did you really think that you an' the marshal could cover your tracks from us?"

In the next instant, Dixon didn't even think. There was no time to think. The threat of Henderson was standing right in front of him now, and he couldn't think.

He had to act. He was spurred on by nothing but pure panic, and the simple will to survive. Dixon acted on pure instinct. Instinct that was driven by countless gunfights that he had participated in. He drew his revolver that had been resting in its holster, on his hip. If you blinked, you would have missed Dixon pulling the gun out. For someone of Dixon's age, he moved with unusual speed, the speed that was honed by the same forces that had shaped his instincts; the pure will to survive anything that a harsh life would throw at him.

Dixon didn't even flinch as he pulled the trigger. The shot rang through the small, enclosed space that was the saloon. At that range, there was no way he was going to miss Dixon. The shot was quick, and the distance very short and manageable. The bullet should have struck Henderson. But somehow it did not.

Dixon blinked several times to confirm what he was seeing. He couldn't believe what had happened. He was definitely old, but he wasn't too old to miss a shot at point blank range. Dixon pointed his gun and fired again at Henderson and still somehow, the shot didn't hit the still-smiling outlaw. He fired again and again, until the chamber in his gun was empty. Dixon couldn't understand how Henderson was still standing despite his desperate barrage of bullets.

Henderson savored the desperation and confusion in Dixon's eyes. He cackled maniacally, taunting the old outlaw who stood in front of him, his mouth agape with shock.

"What;s going on here? How are you still standing? Ain't no man can take all that lead point blank an' still be laughing!"

"Maybe that's what you still don't understand, Dixon. Maybe I'm not a man at all!"

Dixon couldn't understand what Henderson meant. Henderson let out one long maniacal cackle before leaning close to Dixon and saying something. When he spoke, it was only Dixon who heard him. When Dixon heard the much younger outlaw speak, he finally understood everything. When he understood, his heart was filled with terror, and he could do nothing but plead with Henderson.

"No you can't! You can't!" Dixon said.

Henderson chuckled. "Heh. I can, and I will." he said.

Chapter Six: The Things A Girl Can Do

Gruff Garrett struggled to walk straight as he went up the steps of the inn. He tightly gripped the hand rails of the stairs leading to the rented rooms. He took each step carefully as he did not want to lose his balance and trip all over himself on the steps.

Garrett chuckled as he took each step. He struggled to steady his shaky legs and his funny thoughts only made each step, and keeping his balance, even more difficult.

"Heh. Heh. Careful now, old timer. You managed to survive getting shot at by those ornery no accounts back there, you manage NOT to fall off that ledge, and you survive a bear attack. Sure would be a genuine disgrace if you died, by trippin' all over yerself and hitting your head on the stairs. That would be a genuine joke of a death, indeed."

Garrett didn't like the idea at all, and it was that genuine distaste for such an ignominuous death that kept him from falling all over himself. Somehow, he managed to get all the way up to the second floor of the inn, where his rented room was. He passed by Alisa's room, and the door was predictably closed. A passing thought came to Garrett's mind. It was quite a vulgar and distasteful thought, at least to Garrett. He wondered, just for a moment what would happen if he knocked on her door and asked to spend the night with her. Garrett chuckled to himself once again.

"What are you thinkin' old man? You sure are feeling silly tonight. A pretty young an' fetching lady like Alisa would not hesitate to throw you out of her room if you did that. She probably wouldn't even give you the time of day, and I couldn't really blame her for that too."

Garrett silently chided himself for even entertaining such a silly thought, even for a moment. To think that Garrett even carried some hope of getting her attention was downright laughable. Garrett didn't blame himself for feeling this way, of course. Any man young or old would have felt the same way. After all, Alisa was a young and attractive woman, there was no doubt about that. But there was just no way an old man like Gruff Garrett could attract a pretty young lady like Alisa Pemberton. No way, at all.

Garrett chalked up his strange behavior and ideas to the drinks with Dixon, earlier. He had probably drank a lot more than he expected with the old outlaw earlier. That had to be it.

"That was a great meal, but I'll be retiring for the night, Dixon. You should too." Garrett said.

He didn't hear any response from Dixon. Garrett wasn't sure what happened, but he was too tired to care now. Dixon was probably just a little bit slower going up to their rooms. Garrett didn't worry too much about Dixon. He didn't worry at all. After all, Dixon could handle himself and he was so tired, he just wanted to rest.

Garrett opened the door to his room and his eyes fell upon the single bed in the middle of the small room. The bed was neatly fixed with its mattress, sheets and embroidered pillows.

It all looked very inviting.

Garrett almost fell upon the soft sheets and mattress of the bed in his room. It was almost as if his body was pulled onto the mattress like metal being pulled by a magnet. Garett fell onto the mattress and immediately felt the soft and warm comfort it brought. For the longest time, Garrett's bed was the rough outdoors out on the trail. Garrett had almost forgotten the feeling of sleeping on a soft mattress. Once he lay on the bed, Garrett fell into a dreamless sleep almost instantly. His body demanded rest and there was no way it would be denied.

The soft mattress and the inviting dark pulled Garrett in, and he did not want to be pulled out. If it were up to Garrett, he would have wanted to stay in that warm and comfortable dark indefinitely. After all, he was old and he was getting tired of dodging bullets and cheating death. This was all he had known for so many years. Would it be so wrong to demand some rest from it all?

Garrett did not know how long he lay in the darkness. It was so comfortable, that he lost himself in the rest and the nothingness of it all. He couldn't be sure. He also couldn't be sure if the figure that was now pulling him out of the darkness was real, or some wonderful dream he had fallen into. If it were the latter, he didn't want to wake up.

"Hi Gruff."

Garrett recognized the soft and inviting voice anywhere. The sweetness was so distinct and so familiar that Garrett immediately recognized Alisa. Her voice was tender and was very close to him.

Gruff opened his eyes and was surprised to see Alisa standing right in front of him. She was standing in front of Garrett and his eyes almost fell off their sockets. His jaw dropped, and he thought that his tongue might drop to the floor.

Alisa stood in front of Garrett completely naked. He could see her curvaceous body in all its natural splendor. She was naked in front of Garrett, and Alisa was not ashamed at all.

"Alisa... Alisa..."

arrett didn't know what to say, and Alisa didn't let him finish. She moved towards the bed, and promptly lay right beside the old marshal. Garrett was still very confused about all of this, but he did not try to stop her from lying right beside him.

She lay beside him and Garrett felt her soft and supple skin rubbing against his old and coarse flesh. It had been so long since Garrett had felt such a sensation like this before. He had almost forgotten the feeling of a beautiful woman pressed beside him in bed.

It felt like it had been an eternity since this had happened to Gruff again. The truth was, it had only been a few months earlier that Katie Kemp had lay beside him like this. It was a wonderful feeling that Gruff wanted to savor, but the memory of it had been washed away in the horrible trauma of her tragic and premature death. Garrett had buried the feeling deep inside of him, and he had never even dared hope to feel this kind of sensation again, much less with Alisa. Now, she was lying beside him, and his seemingly unlikely fantasies were coming to life in front of him.

Garrett couldn't help but feel a rush of excitement mix in with the pleasurable sensation of lying beside Alisa. Electricity seemed to buzz in and out of his skin when they brushed against each other. This moment seemed to good to be true, and Garrett simply couldn't believe it.

"Alisa, what are you doing here? Good gracious."

Alisa chuckled and pressed a soft finger to Garrett's lips." "What do you think I'm doing? I'm lying beside you. I want to be with you tonight."

"Good Lord almighty, this is a dream. This just has to be a dream." Garrett said.

Alisa shook her head. "Ain't no dream, Gruff. This is all very real an' it's happening now."

Garrett blinked and rubbed his eyes. This only seemed to amuse Alisa even more, who pressed even closer to him. Despite himself, Garrett,

couldn't help but feel excited and pleasurable at the same time now.

Alisa giggled again and touched Gruff on his exposed arm. He felt the slight tingle of electricity buzzing through his arm. It was a very pleasant sensation, and it reassured Gruff even as he was still confused.

"Alisa..."

Garrett hesitated before speaking. He didn't know if what he would say would hurt Alisa, but he respected her too much not to say it.

"Alisa have you so easily forgotten what... what..."

Even then, Garrett hesitated to finish. He knew that the memory of what Alisa had been through was still very fresh in her mind. He knew that she was still hurting from it, and understandably so. He didn't want to open up any old wounds but he didn't know how else to say what he needed to say.

"Have I forgotten what those god awful no accounts done to me? Of course not, Gruff. You don't need to hesitate to say it. I know an' it's all right."

Garrett was relieved when Alisa put his fears and doubts to rest. However, it still didn't explain any of this, and what she was trying to do.

"I'm glad to hear that, but I still don't understand why yer... yer right here, lying beside me."

"You don't like it?" Alisa asked.

"I didn't say I didn't like it, Lord no! Any man would... would welcome something like this... and well... well..."

Garrett struggled with the right words to say, and

Alisa giggled like a little girl. She was amused at how the old lawman stammered and struggled with how to explain himself. "Alisa you are one very attractive woman. Of that, there can be no doubt at all. I am very attracted to you. But you do know that I'm old. I'm old enough to be yer grandfather. Maybe even great grandfather! And yer young and pretty and beautiful. You've got yer whole life ahead of ya! You do know it ain't well.. it ain't proper for an old geezer like myself and you to... to..."

Alisa shook her head and smiled at Gruff. She kept her eyes on him, not once wavering or looking away. Her eyes had a soft and inviting look to them. Garrett knew that she was quietly inviting and welcoming him with just her stare.

"Come on now, Gruff. We both know that I'm old enough to do whatever I want. And yes, I know that we have a huge age gap. And yes, I do still remember what those buzzards did to me. I ain't ever going to forget that."

It was only then, that a hint of anger returned in

Alisa's eyes. Garrett immediately detected it, and he was sorry that he might have reminded her of what had happened.

"Alisa, I'm sorry. I didn't mean to open up old wounds or anything."

Alisa shook her head and touched Garrett lightly on his ear. He felt that strong buzz of electricity again, and she was almost irresistible to him now.

"You don't got nothing to apologize for, Gruff. I ain't you that done such a horrible deed to me. Believe me, I ain't got nuthin' but respect and care for you in my heart. But don't worry. I'm not here to make love with you. I know what you're saying."

Garrett's eyes widened, and he gave Alisa a puzzled look.

"What do you mean you're not going to make love to me?" Alisa giggled like an amused little girl trying to explain something to an old dog. In a way, that was exactly how it was.

"Do I detect more than a little hint of disappointment in yer voice, Gruff?"

Gruff hesitated and stammered out a reply. "Well, I... I mean... I... I don't..."

"Don't try so hard to figure it out, old timer. You don't need to wrap your head around it too much if it hurts. I'm not going to make love to you tonight, but there are still a lot of things a girl can do to make a man feel good other than what yer thinking. And I know a lot of them things. I know 'em well."

Garrett heard Alisa and he simply closed his eyes. He could see her point clearly now. There was no reason for him to resist or even try to convince her not to do any of this. No man in the same situation would have done otherwise. Alisa was simply too attractive. This was simply a case of the grass moving towards the horse. There was no reason for the horse not to take a bite anymore.

Gruff savored the moment and enjoyed it. He felt Alisa right beside him now. Their skin was touching against each other, and it felt very right. He felt her kiss him on the lips and he simply obliged. It had been so long since he felt a woman's lips on his, and he had been through so much. This was simply a wonderful and welcome release. Garrett simply accepted what was in front of him now.

Garrett felt Alisa embrace him, and he held her tight. Unlike before, Garrett did not feel Alisa tremble in fear at his embrace. He did not feel any ounce of fear from her. This time, he was not hugging a young woman that had just been ravaged by several outlaws. He was not holding a young woman trembling in fear. He was holding a young woman that felt nothing but security and gratitude in his arms. He held tightly a young woman who trusted him completely and knew that he would protect her no matter what. Garrett himself, felt that Alisa simply wanted to show that gratitude and give him some tender care tonight. After everything they had been through, it was just what he needed.

Gruff held Alisa tightly in his arms. He had kissed her, and she had kissed him. They had felt their bodies close to each other, and both of them felt safe and secure. Garrett savored the tender moment with her. He wanted to hold the moment tightly, just as tightly as he held Alisa now. This was the first moment in a long time that

Garrett felt safe and secure. It was the first moment in a long time, that bullets weren't flying, and Garrett's life, or someone's he cared for wasn't in danger. For the first time in almost an eternity, Garrett's chest was clear. There was no pounding of his damaged heart, no stress and tension, and his breathing was deep and relaxed. For the first time in a long while,

Garrett didn't feel like death was just around the corner, or just at his heels. For the first time in a long while, Garrett felt like he was truly living.

"Alisa..." Garrett whispered.

"What is it, Gruff?"

Garrett was surprised that Alisa answered him. He thought that she had already dozed off to sleep.

"Can't... can't we stay in this moment, forever? Can't we do that?" he said.

Alisa mumbled something of a response. It seemed Alisa was half asleep now, and Garrett couldn't be sure of exactly what she said. Whatever she said, Alisa did sound pleasant and content. Garrett could feel her breathing. It was steady and consistent along with the beating of her heart. That was enough of a response for Garrett and he smiled and closed his eyes.

Garrett was already feeling himself falling into a peaceful and content sleep. He was losing consciousness and welcoming the dark, but there was no fear and exhaustion now in his heart. There was only peace and contentment. It wasn't going to last. It was just as Garrett had said. If only they could make this moment last forever.

Just as Garrett was about to lose consciousness and fall asleep, he felt himself being pulled back up to consciousness. This time, he wasn't being pulled back up pleasantly, like it was with Alisa. He was being pulled back up forcefully, in a very unpleasant manner.

Garrett heard the sound of several knocks on his door. The knocks were loud and forceful. They were desperate and would not stop until they were heard.

Garrett and even Alisa were half-asleep and could not get up to answer the loud knocks. There was no way they were going to get up, unless something more forceful was used to rouse them.

Paolo Dixon kicked the door down and the sound finally roused Garrett and Alisa with a start. They both almost bolted out of bed and saw Dixon standing in front of them.

"Dixon! What are you doing?" Garrett said.

Dixon had a desperate look in his eye. He had seen Garrett and Alisa lying together, but he didn't care. He only cared about telling them what he knew. His voice trembled even as he almost yelled at them.

"We got to get out of here! Henderson and his men are going to kill my daughter!" Dixon said.